I0749226

THE FORGOTTEN GAME

TAHIR SHAH

KOK KAR YING

THE FORGOTTEN GAME

TAHIR SHAH

KOK KAR YING

MMXXIII

Secretum Mundi Publishing Ltd
124 City Road
London
EC1V 2NX
United Kingdom

www.secretum-mundi.com
info@secretum-mundi.com

First published by Secretum Mundi Publishing Ltd, 2023

THE FORGOTTEN GAME

Artwork drawn by Kok Kar Ying

A CIP catalogue record for this title is available from the British Library.

ISBN 978-1-914960-94-9

VERSION 24012023

Visit the author's website:
Tahirshah.com

Once upon a time there was a land called Opopicot, ruled by a compassionate king, where games were unknown.

The people were educated and well fed,
but they had never been exposed to
games of any kind.

The reason was that, in antiquity, one of the king's distant ancestors had despised games because he hated losing.

And so, by royal decree, he had ordered for all games to be banned on pain of death.

Centuries had passed since then and, as the kingdom was cut off from much of the outside world, no one ever had cause to hear about games, let alone play them.

One day, in a distant corner of the kingdom, an impoverished farmer was ploughing his field, as he did from morning till night.

The farmer’s plough suddenly struck an object.

It was hard and apparently large.

Assuming it to be a rock of some kind, the farmer leaned down, and dug away with his hands.

All of a sudden, he realized that he hadn't struck a rock at all, but a wooden chest…

…a chest fastened shut
with a rusted iron padlock.

Hoping for a golden treasure, the farmer dug the box out, knocked off the lock with a stone and, cautiously, drew back the lid.

Inside, there was treasure,
but not the kind the farmer was expecting.

Instead of gold coins, he discovered a large square-shaped board made from black and white marble.

The squares were checkered light and dark…

…and inlaid around the edges
of the board were precious gems.

In a leather pouch beside the board,
the old farmer found a number
of exquisitely carved figures.

Like the board, some were dark and others light, all of them inset with precious stones.

Delighted at having stumbled upon a treasure, the farmer immediately thought about how he would sell it and make some money.

At that moment, a group of soldiers from the royal guard were passing.

Noticing the farmer and the chest,
they hurried over to see what was going on.

Within hours, the farmer and the contents of the chest had been taken to the palace, where the King of Opopicot was holding court in the throne room.

Bowing and stooping, the farmer described what had occurred – how his plough had struck the chest.

The monarch inspected the curious checkered board and the exquisitely carved pieces.

Having rewarded the farmer with
a fistful of gold, he took possession
of the unusual discovery.

Whenever dignitaries visited the palace, the king wasted no time in showing off the objects.

Everyone who set eyes on them was amazed at the workmanship.

Years passed.

Even though the king came across many other exquisite objects, the board and pieces held a special place in the throne room, and in his heart.

One morning, when the king was aged,
a young prince arrived at the palace, hoping
to win the hand of the royal princess,
whose name was Jihane.

She was so lovely that a stream of princes and suitors constantly arrived in the hope of wooing her.

All were turned away because they could not pass the test, which was to observe the world in a new and unexpected way.

Now, it just so happened that while he was waiting to be received, the handsome young prince got chatting to an equerry in an ornately decorated salon that led on to the throne room.

In hushed tones, the equerry informed the young prince that the object displayed on a special table had been the king's pride and joy since it had been unearthed by a humble farmer many years before.

Marvelling at the craftsmanship,
the prince smiled.
'Does His Majesty like to play?' he asked.

The equerry frowned.
'*Play*? Play what?'
'Play the game of chess, of course.'

‘You must be mistaken,’ the equerry snapped. ‘This is a prized object, sacred to the realm, and is not connected to anything as asinine as a game!’

Just then, the doors to the throne room swung open and the young prince was ushered inside.

Finding himself face to face with the monarch, he was asked to provide an example of seeing the world in a new and unexpected way.

Hopeful to gain the hand of the king's
favourite daughter, the prince swallowed hard.

'Hurry!' hissed the vizier from behind the throne. 'His Majesty dislikes being kept waiting!'

Again, the king demanded an example of observing the world in a new and unexpected way.

Again, the prince swallowed hard.
And again, the vizier hissed.

The king clicked his fingers, indicating for the suitor to be flung out on his ear.

Instantly, a pair of burly
guards lurched forwards.

Grasping hold of the prince,
they spun him around.

Just as the suitor was about to be dragged from the throne room, he spied the ornate chess set through the doorway.

‘What a wonderful chess set!’
he exclaimed at the top of his lungs.

The king cocked his head.
'Stop!'

The guards dropped the young suitor,
who clambered to his feet.

‘*Set*?’ the monarch boomed. ‘What do you mean – *set*?’

The prince motioned out to the anteroom.

'The set you have out there. It's absolutely glorious. I should imagine that His Majesty plays very well.'

The king grunted hard.
'Play *what* well?' he hissed.

‘Why, chess, of course.’

His curiosity piqued, the ruler of the kingdom was unable to prevent himself from enquiring what chess was about.

And, within moments of first hearing the name, he was learning the rules…

. . . the rules of a game that is
of course so terribly easy to grasp
but so dastardly difficult to master.

Needless to say, in the hours that followed, the prince taught the king basic chess strategies.

The monarch was thrilled by
what he had learned, and by the fact that
something so lovely to look at could have
another use – one that challenged the mind
in the most profound ways.

The prince won the hand of Princess Jihane, and everyone lived happily ever after.

And that is the end of our tale.

Except, it's not quite the end.

You see, stories like this one
both amuse and delight.

But their power is even greater.

Given the right conditions,
they work on our unconscious mind,
passing on ideas and information –
teaching us from the inside out.

In the same way that the game of chess was relearned in the Kingdom of Opopicot, we can relearn to see what we think we know in new ways…

…to perceive layers that are
inaudible to our ears…

…and invisible to our eyes…

…the secret layers of stories.

Finis

About the Author

Descended from a long line of storytellers, writers, and savants, Tahir Shah is one of the most prolific authors of his generation. He has published more than sixty books in numerous genres, including travel, fiction, and fantasy, as well as tales for children.

Raised in the tradition of Eastern 'teaching stories', Shah is passionate about stories and storytelling. He regards the ability to learn from folklore as being in us all, what he calls a 'default setting of humankind'. As well as having written scores of books, Shah has made documentaries for National Geographic TV and The History Channel. He is the founder and CEO of the charity, The Scheherazade Foundation.

About the Artist

Kok Kar Ying is a passionate illustrator from Malaysia who creates art by adapting and experimenting with a variety of traditional and digital media. Her aim is to bring authors' words to life with creative compositions and highly detailed artworks. She has experience in illustrating children's books and educational materials.

Books By Tahir Shah

Travel

Trail of Feathers
Travels With Myself
Beyond the Devil's Teeth
In Search of King Solomon's Mines
House of the Tiger King
In Arabian Nights
The Caliph's House
Sorcerer's Apprentice
Journey Through Namibia

Novels

Jinn Hunter: Book One – The Prism
Jinn Hunter: Book Two – The Jinnslayer
Jinn Hunter: Book Three – The Perplexity
Hannibal Fogg and the Supreme Secret of Man
Hannibal Fogg and the Codex Cartographica
Casablanca Blues
Eye Spy
Godman
Paris Syndrome
Timbuctoo

Nasrudin

Travels With Nasrudin
The Misadventures of the Mystifying Nasrudin
The Peregrinations of the Perplexing Nasrudin
The Voyages and Vicissitudes of Nasrudin
Nasrudin in the Land of Fools

Teaching Stories

The Arabian Nights Adventures

Scorpion Soup

Tales Told to a Melon

The Afghan Notebook

The Caravanserai Stories

Ghoul Brothers

Hourglass

Imaginist

Jinn's Treasure

Jinnlore

Mellified Man

Skeleton Island

Wellspring

When the Sun Forgot to Rise

Outrunning the Reaper

The Cap of Invisibility

On Backgammon Time

The Wondrous Seed

The Paradise Tree

Mouse House

The Hoopoe's Flight

The Old Wind

A Treasury of Tales

Daydreams of an Octopus & Other Stories

Miscellaneous

The Reason to Write

Zigzag Think

Being Myself

Research

Cultural Research

The Middle East Bedside Book

Three Essays

Anthologies

The Anthologies

The Clockmaker's Box

The Tahir Shah Fiction Reader

The Tahir Shah Travel Reader

Edited by

Congress With a Crocodile

A Son of a Son, Volume I

A Son of a Son, Volume II

Screenplays

Casablanca Blues: The Screenplay

Timbuctoo: The Screenplay

A REQUEST

If you enjoyed this book, please review it on your favourite online retailer or review website.

Reviews are an author's best friend.

To stay in touch with Tahir Shah, and to hear about his upcoming releases before anyone else, please sign up for his mailing list:

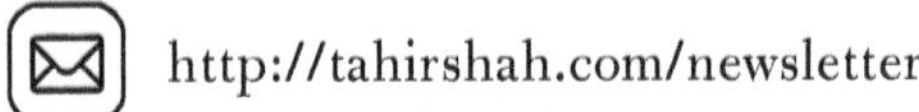

And to follow him on social media, please go to any of the following links:

http://www.twitter.com/humanstew

@tahirshah999

http://www.facebook.com/TahirShahAuthor

http://www.youtube.com/user/tahirshah999

http://www.pinterest.com/tahirshah

https://www.goodreads.com/tahirshahauthor

http://www.tahirshah.com

www.ingramcontent.com/pod-product-compliance
Lightning Source LLC
Chambersburg PA
CBHW030523310726
48979CB00010B/1778/J
* 9 7 8 1 9 1 4 9 6 0 9 4 9 *